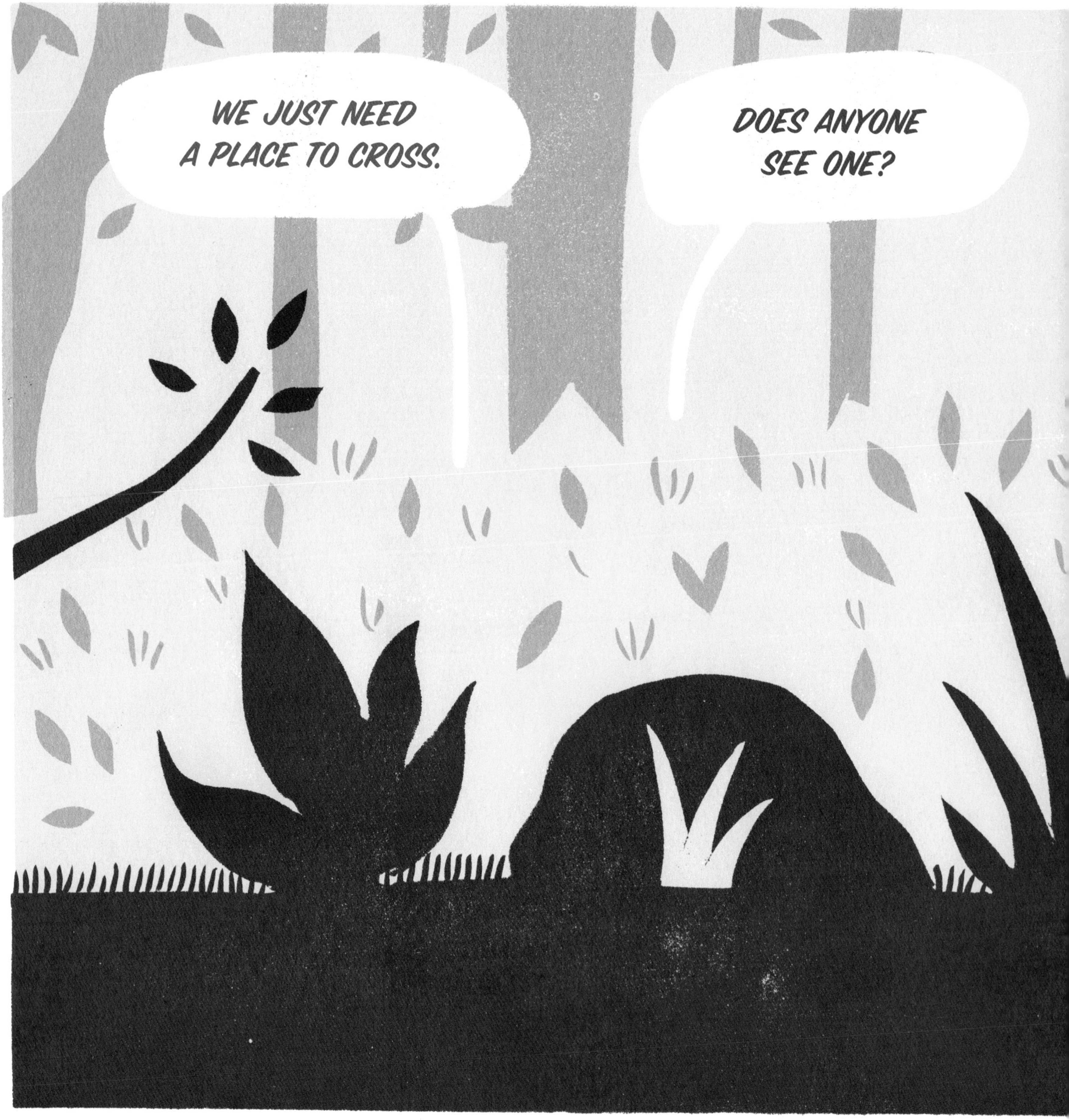
WE JUST NEED A PLACE TO CROSS.
DOES ANYONE SEE ONE?

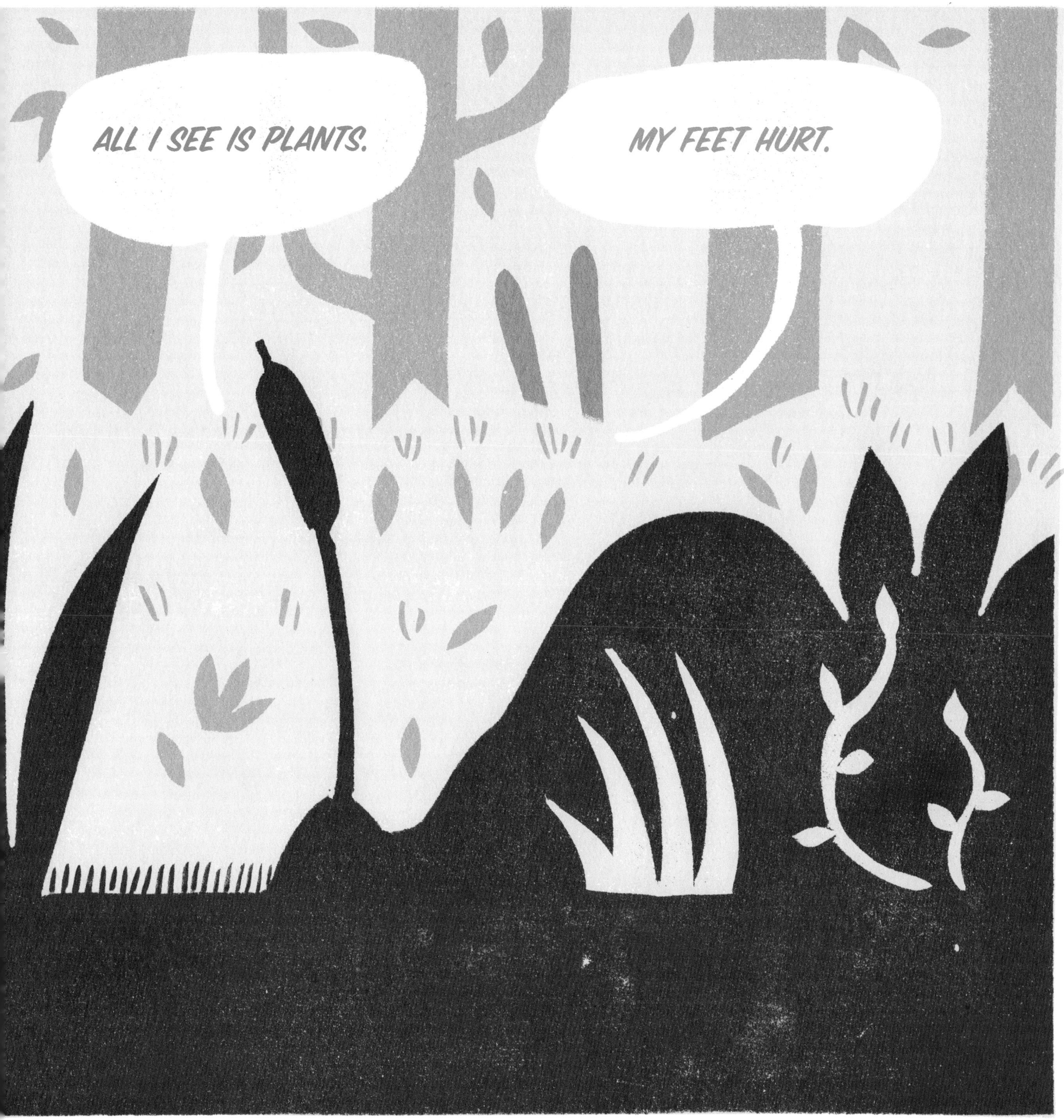
ALL I SEE IS PLANTS.
MY FEET HURT.

FOR JEROME
—JARRETT

FOR JARRETT
—JEROME

For information about permission to reproduce selections from this book, write to
Permissions, W. W. Norton & Company, Inc., 500 Fifth Avenue, New York, NY 10110

For information about special discounts for bulk purchases, please contact W. W. Norton
Special Sales at specialsales@wwnorton.com or 800-233-4830

Manufacturing by Phoenix Color • Production manager: Julia Druskin

Library of Congress Cataloging-in-Publication Data

Names: Pumphrey, Jarrett, author, illustrator. | Pumphrey, Jerome, author, illustrator. • Title: Somewhere in the bayou / [by] Jarrett
Pumphrey [and] Jerome Pumphrey. • Description: First edition. | New York : Norton Young Readers, an imprint of W. W. Norton and
Company, [2022] | Audience: Ages 4–8. | Summary: Opossum, Squirrel, Rabbit, and Mouse want to cross the bayou, but next to the
log they are considering as a bridge is a sneaky tail, which may be attached to someone dangerous—each of the four approach the
problem with a different strategy, with varying results. • Identifiers: LCCN 2021016239 | ISBN 9781324015932 (hardcover) | ISBN
9781324015949 (epub) • Subjects: LCSH: Animals—Juvenile fiction. | Bayous—Juvenile fiction. | Problem solving—Juvenile fiction. |
Picture books for children. | CYAC: Bayous—Fiction. | Animals—Fiction. | Problem solving—Fiction. | LCGFT: Picture books.Classification:
LCC PZ7.P97328 So 2022 | DDC 813.6 [E]—dc23 • LC record available at https://lccn.loc.gov/2021016239

W. W. Norton & Company, Inc., 500 Fifth Avenue, New York, N.Y. 10110 • www.wwnorton.com

W. W. Norton & Company Ltd., 15 Carlisle Street, London W1D 3BS

0 9 8 7 6 5 4 3 2 1

Jarrett Pumphrey   Jerome Pumphrey

SOMEWHERE
in the
BAYOU

 Norton Young Readers • An Imprint of W. W. Norton and Company • Independent Publishers Since 1923

LET'S CROSS HERE.
WAIT. WHAT'S THAT?
THAT'S A TAIL.
THAT'S A SNEAKY TAIL.

THAT'S A SCARY TAIL!

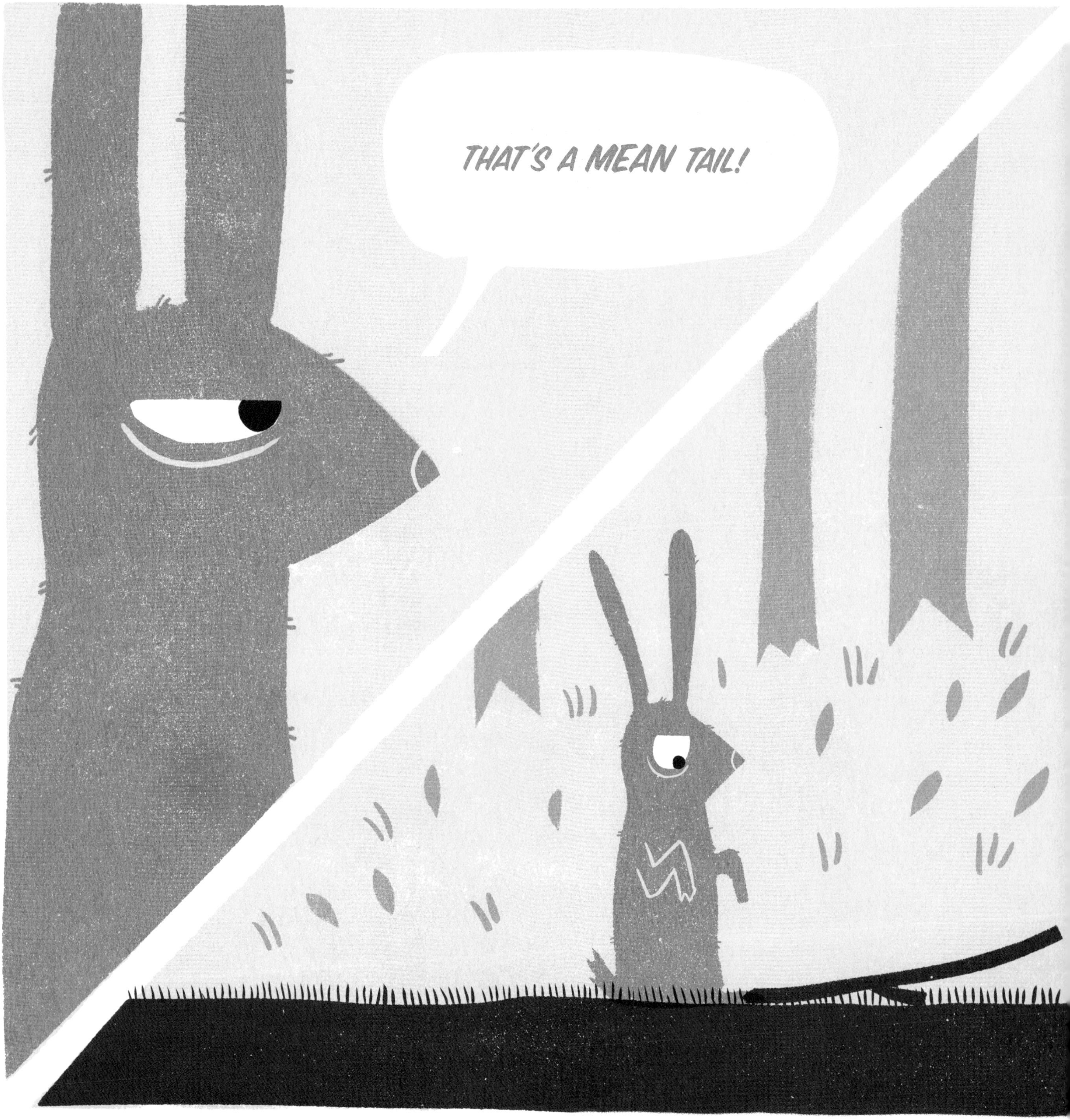
THAT'S A MEAN TAIL!

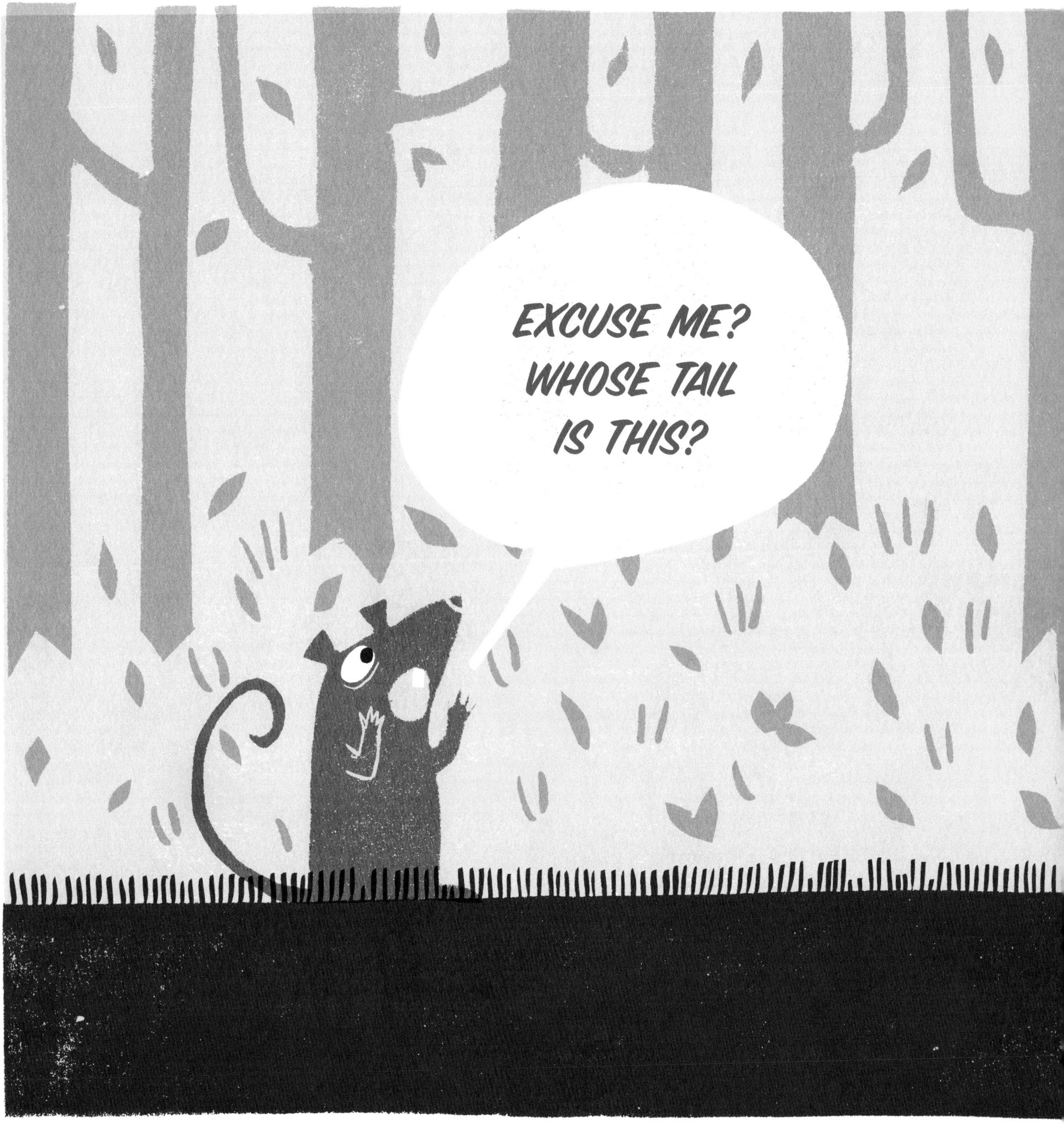
EXCUSE ME?
WHOSE TAIL
IS THIS?

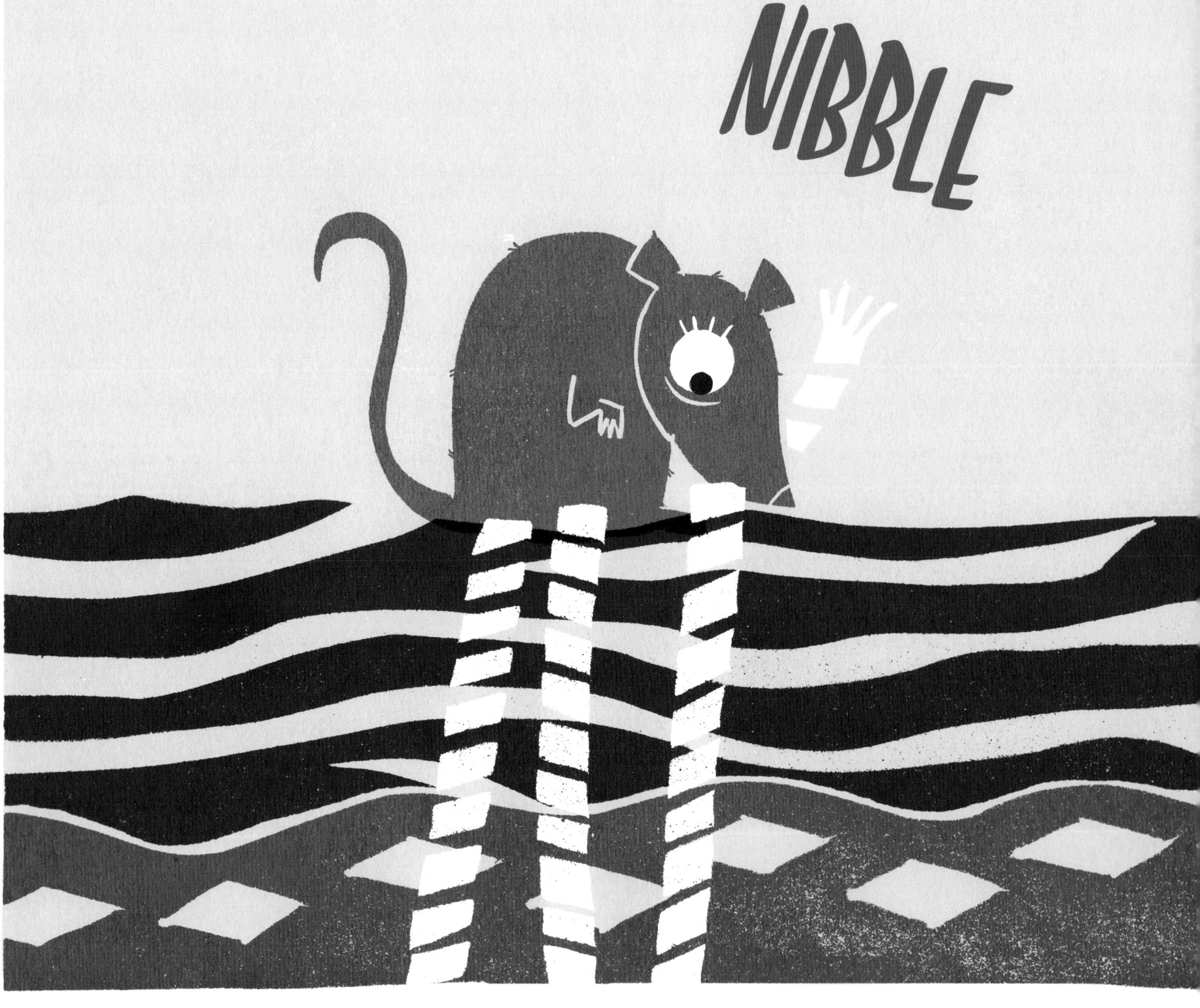
NIBBLE

OH . . . UH . . .
YOU'RE WELCOME.